Of
Heroes,
Hooks, and
Heirlooms

D0066742

Of Heroes, Hooks, and Heirlooms

by Faye Silton

THE JEWISH PUBLICATION SOCIETY
Philadelphia • Jerusalem

The Jewish Publication Society
1930 Chestnut Street
Philadelphia, PA 19103

Manufactured in the United States of America

Library of Congress Cataloging-in-Publication Data

Silton, Faye
    Of heroes, hooks, and heirlooms / by Faye Silton.
        p. cm.
    Summary: Twelve-year-old Mia, the daughter of
Holocaust survivors, learns to crochet so she can make a lace
collar like the one her grandmother is wearing in the family's
only surviving photograph.
    ISBN 0–8276–0582–X [Hard cover]
        0–8276–0649–4 [Paper cover]
    [1. Holocaust survivors—Fiction. 2. Jews—Fiction.
    3. Crocheting—Fiction.] 1. Title.
PZ7, S586530f 1996
[Fic] —dc20   96-24497
                                                  CIP
                                                  AC

To my parents,
Dora Lieder Goldsmith
and Frederick F. Goldsmith,
the ultimate heroes

Contents

Of Heroes, Hooks, and Heirlooms

1

It would happen on a visit to New York City. The roar of the subway train would not drown out my everyday prayer, "Today, please God, let me find her for my mother."

I would step into the hot train, grab a pole in the center of the car, and scan the passengers, from one end to the other. I know what to look for: Mom's Mutti had high cheekbones, small, sleepy, light eyes, very sad. She would be staring straight ahead. She would wear old clothes and maybe move with pain.

And, oh, this is the part I pray for the hardest: I would catch sight of her, and, carefully working my way back to her seat, strap to strap, I would step closer, careful not to frighten her because she has been afraid for such a long time.

"I am Mia, your grandchild."

"I not understand," she would pull back in fright anyway.

Then I would look straight into her eyes and explain, my hand on her arm.

"Tonia. I am Tonia's daughter and I will bring you to Tonia. She cries for you all the time."

The train would scream to the next stop and, carefully, carefully, my arm linked in hers, we would cross the platform and return home. My mother would stare in disbelief and then whisper, "My *gebenschte kind!* My blessed child!"

She would smile again and I would be a hero.

More than anything else, I want to be a hero. My parents are heroes because they survived Hitler's war and started a family all over again. Even some of the kids in school qualify as heroes. Just last week, Brian phoned the ambulance service with precise information that saved a life. Last winter, Frank plunged into Frog Pond to save an ice-skating buddy on an eighth-grade field trip. I just want to help my Mom be less sad, to make up to her something of what she lost.

Long before we began the Heritage Project in school, I already knew our family was not like any other in the neighborhood. I don't mean that no one else kept the Sabbath as strictly as we did (although that was true), or that no one else's parents said, "It's better maybe not to shine too much, not to wear red, not to be the best."

No one else's parents spoke with heavy European accents and, except for a few needy people who ate with us on the Sabbath and at holiday times, we had no guests: no grandparents, no cozy evenings spent talking about the good, old days with laughter and tears. Well, that's not exactly true. There were tears. During the Passover Seder when we chant, "Pour out your wrath...." and include an additional paragraph in memory of those who died in the Holocaust, Mom would stare at our only old photograph on the dining room wall. Her eyes would swell and redden, and even Dad would flick away a tear from under the glint of his glasses.

For many years after the war, there were small pieces of stories. Mom had no proof that Mutti had actually died. The doubt about Mutti was my best hope. If she had survived and left Europe, she would probably have ended up in New York City, as did so many immigrants, at least for a time. If she lived and worked there, she would have no car. So she would use the subway.

But one day a fat letter arrived from Cousin Marta in England. She had "come out" alive despite the terror. She had, with her own eyes, "seen Mutti and the little ones shot."

Mom sat at our kitchen table, in her purple, printed house dress, clutching at her blond hair, coughing and weeping. On the table was the framed photo that she gazed at during the Passover Seder.

"What is it, Mom? What has happened?"

"*Also*," she finally said in German. "So then, this photo is all that is left of them."

My father stood behind her and rubbed her shoulders, his eyes small and moist. Then Mom laid her head on the photo and took great, shuddering breaths. Later that night my father called the doctor.

(Front, left to right: Mutti; Mia's mother, Tonia; Papa.
Back: Mia's two uncles, Kurt and Felix.)

"Your wife has developed pneumonia over a broken heart. Take care with her," the doctor warned.

My father and I ached for Mom, whose last hope had died with the letter from Marta. Mutti, she wrote, was shot to death outside Lublin, Poland, where the Nazis had held frightened, frozen, and starving Jews penned up in a ghetto, filthy with disease.

Mom had grown stronger since that terrible day, but almost overnight, her hair turned completely white. More than a few of the kids in school asked, "Is that your Mom, the lady in white, who sits in the window of the dry-cleaning shop, sewing?"

This is my parents' story. My dad manages the cleaning and laundry part of the shop. I think it smells terrible, but he says the odor of clean chemicals is marvelous compared with the stench and filth of the ghettos and camps during the war. He likes the idea of taking crumpled, filthy things and restoring them to their former glory—smooth, crisp and clean.

He told me that Mom survived the camps because she was a genius with a needle and thread, making beautiful things—evening gowns and suits for the Nazi officers, their wives, and girl friends. It's real handy for Dad to have her repair garments for his customers right here in the shop.

Sometimes, though, customers never come back for their cleaning. After a year or so, Mom cuts the clothing into colorful shapes and sews gorgeous patchwork bags from the cloth. Now Dad decorates the shop with her bags and everyone wants to buy them. Usually Mom is shy and hardly talks at all. But here is the problem: She asks every bag customer the same question, "And what will you take in it? What will you put in?"

I think this question, more than her pale, ghostly appearance, makes my friends wonder at her strangeness. I've never told them what I learned from overheard snatches of conversations— how when she was twelve, just my age, the storm troopers kicked in her door.

"*Los, Los!*" They shrieked. "Pack one bag, each of you, and get out!"

The family spent most of the hour agonizing about what to pack for deportation. Mom packed her father's medicines and still he died. Mutti packed her Sabbath candlesticks and still she did not survive. Her brother took food, prayer book, tefillin, and underwear in his bag, and still he died. In the end, all those bags were snatched from them. Now *things* matter little to Mom. She often says, "Things like clothes and furniture aren't very important, darling. They took all our things during the war in Europe. Only our ideas and skills they couldn't take."

But still she asks the question. It torments her: "What will you put in this bag?"

Maybe she still thinks that a better choice of things *would* have made a difference.

In a way, all of this weird stuff makes me special in school. But that bothers me, too. What I want is to be special because of something I do or am—that hero stuff again.

I've never told my friends about nights in our home. How my mother wakes up sweating and shaking. Sometimes she even screams. And my father rocks her like a child in his arms till she is quiet and finally falls asleep again.

I don't dare ask why this happens, but it must be that she was so frightened and tortured when she was younger that she can't help but dream of it. She also hoards groceries—canned beans, sacks of flour, dry milk and rice, though there are only three of us and food stores all around our neighborhood. In her mind, Dad says, she is still sifting through dirt for meager potatoes and beets. She must still feel hungry.

I would feel plenty heroic if I could make her better, make both Mom and Dad happier, do something that would matter.

I guess I can understand how, after they lost so much, my parents would be careful to live simply. We eat a thin slice of rye bread with a soft egg for breakfast every morning. And each morning, I button on a plain, white blouse and step into a navy blue or brown skirt. On the Sabbath there is a navy jumper and a fresh white blouse to wear to synagogue. Plainest and clumsiest of all are my tie-on oxfords that Dad polishes to a high sheen just before the Sabbath.

Even our apartment aches with drabness. Mom's purple print house dress is the happiest color in the apartment. All the rest melts into a beigeness that I can understand but cannot abide.

Probably it was my hunger for color that eventually drew me to The Noble

Needle yarn shop just a block from my school. Every day I passed it, wishing I had money to spend, and then, finally, I wished for the courage to go in without the money! One day I did.

In that magical shop, jewel colors cascaded from ceiling to floor. Here and there sample sweaters studded the walls for the window shopper's amazement. Soft yarn balls filled straw baskets on the floor, and net hammocks floated from the rafters.

I walked in.

"Can I help you?" asked a gray-haired lady seated with a cloud of pale blue mohair in her lap. She stood up carefully and the mohair slipped into a basket at her feet.

"Do you knit or crochet? Which do you prefer?"

"Oh no," I answered as I looked around the room. "But I love these colors. I'd love to touch them."

She laughed. Kindly, though.

"Of course, you can. I think you would like crochet. Believe it or not, I've made all these things with a simple crochet hook—what I call the ... 'noble needle.' "

I shook my head. "My mother is good with a needle—a sewing needle—but I am probably all thumbs, and I have no money for yarn."

"Look," she said as she held her hand out to me. "I am Irene and you are... from the people at the dry cleaners, no?"

"Yes, I'm Mia," I said.

"On Mondays I usually need help unpacking the shipments and finding places for the yarns. I can't stretch like I used to. You could help me and I could help you."

Then she reached over to a basket of soft, bright colors and held it out to me as if she were offering fruit.

"These are odd lots of yarn left over

from various projects and customers. Choose something that you like and we'll start right now."

Only in America, Mom would have said. I was speechless.

There was a ball of buttery yellow, delicate and downy, another of brick red, fuzzy and bright, and royal purple flecked with navy.

"Choose something smooth for your first project so you can clearly see the stitches,," she suggested, as her fingers combed through a pile of colorful needles, checking their girth and smoothness.

I picked the purple, and she coiled a loop around her finger, popped it over the head of the hook, and in seconds worked a chain a foot long.

"Here, you try it." She covered my hand with her soft, swollen one. In moments we tried building on the chain, tall double, even triple crochet. Clumsy,

I tried to follow. My work looked bumpy, even knotty, but Irene wasn't perturbed.

"Crochet is wonderful because you can pull it right out if you make a mistake. Here, try again."

After a few tries, I actually did it. Irene suggested working with a fat yarn and fat needle for the first day. She showed me how to skip stitches and form clusters, creating a kind of lace.

"For Monday," she said, "we'll make a pillow—just two squares, and we'll do something marvelous with it. Is it a deal?"

I just nodded, speechless with joy.

Then she packed everything into a sleek, shopping bag, imprinted with the name of her store, The Noble Needle. The bag bumped against my knees as I rushed home to help prepare for the Sabbath. There was so much I could do. My pillow would liven up the bare sofa. I could make seat covers for the chairs, even a challah cover!

M agical Monday finally arrived. I
was so excited about going back to
Irene and The Noble Needle that in history class I didn't pay much attention to
Mrs. Searle and her "ancestor hunt."

For weeks we had talked about Ellis
Island, where so many immigrants
arrived to step, at last, onto American
soil. Then she reminded us how sad it is
that some of us are so far apart from our
roots. She thought it would be wonderful to reforge those links with the past.

"Our first step," she explained, "is to

find out about your roots. Here is a
blank family tree. Take it home and go
back as far as you can. But, more impor-
tantly, start with yourself, then your parents, grandparents, and so on."

The paper burned in my hand. How
could I ask them? How could I ask Mom
and Dad to fill out a tree that had lost so
many of its branches?

Sharon, in the last row, raised her
hand.

"But, Mrs. Searle, what if many in
the family have died? A number of people in my father's family have heart
problems, so several have died. It would
be painful to ask Dad to fill this out."

I could have kissed her. Mrs. Searle
rested her cheek on her hand for a
moment.

"That's a tough one, Sharon. But,
you know, psychologists tell us that
when a dear one dies, the family wants
friends to ask about him or her. It means

that the one who died has made some kind of mark, left a trace of himself. The relatives are hit hard, but they like knowing that others notice the empty spot too. Why not leave this on your kitchen table and ask your mother if she would mind filling it out as well as she can? It may not be as terrible as you imagine."

I thought I would do the same.

This is what actually happened when I brought the papers home. In his fine, spidery handwriting, Dad filled out his half of the tree. Mom just shook her head.

"I don't remember. I don't remember anything."

So her side was blank. My tree was the only one that looked this strange. That old feeling again. Weird.

But the next day there was a new assignment, still more difficult. Mrs. Searle wanted to teach us "photoanalysis" before we finished the Heritage Project with the Heirloom Fair. Now I really shook myself to attention and raised my hand.

"What exactly happens at an Heirloom Fair?"

"Not to worry. You will each need to bring in a family heirloom and tell a story about it at an evening presentation. All parents are welcome, and we will serve exotic refreshments afterwards.

An heirloom! Well, there was absolutely nothing I could bring. Nothing. More pressing yet was the photoanalysis project. I glanced around the class. Everyone was listening intently. My palms were already sweaty.

"Photos," Mrs. Searle continued, "are mirrors with memories. You've all got boxes full of photographs, yellowed with age. Bring in several. We will have an expert help you do some detective work. You will be amazed at what you can learn from old pictures."

Mrs. Searle would be amazed that my family had only one photo, brown-tinged, which showed five very serious people.

After school, when I got to The Noble Needle, Irene sensed that something was wrong.

"What is it, Mia? Today you seem not yourself."

"It's school. We're working on a heritage project and have to bring in heirlooms for a presentation in two weeks. Our family doesn't have heirlooms. During the war they were chased from their homes and the small bundles strapped on their backs were snatched from them by Nazi soldiers."

"Two weeks, you say. We'll think of something. But today we will crochet after you've unpacked these boxes of mohair. You decide how to arrange the colors."

The work was wonderful in Irene's store. It was like painting with a whole palette of colors and no messy clean-up. Later, my crochet hook became a magic wand, flicking in and out of the yarn scraps. Inches of scarlet, purple, and teal spilled over my lap while Irene waited on customers. The swatch could become a scarf or even a baby afghan, but today it would be a pillow cover— just what our plain, old sofa at home needed. I imagined colorful, woolly scarves hanging on hooks near the door in our apartment, scarves that I could crochet.

Too soon it was time to leave.

"Perhaps your mother can help you sew the pillow cover together. I know her work. I have one of her exquisite bags right here."

I wondered if my mom had asked Irene her usual, "And what will you put in?" What must Irene think of her?

What did she know about our family?

"Take some balls with you. Try something on your own and we'll talk more next time," Irene said as she filled my bag with small balls of red, yellow, navy and purple mohair.

That night, with the colorful yarn balls scattered over my bed, I invented a narrow tie as long as any man's tie. Because it was so narrow, the rows were short and quick. I finished it in an hour. It would really cheer up my plain, white blouse and navy skirt. I couldn't wait to go to school to surprise everyone. But more pressing was the assignment for the "ancestor hunt."

How could I ask my parents to lend me their only photo? What if it got bent or I lost it? Worse yet, I couldn't upset them the way they were upset each Passover as they stared at that picture. Most of all, I couldn't ask for an heirloom to borrow for the fair. There wasn't one.

To remind them would be cruel.

Actually, bringing things into school has always been a problem. Even in kindergarten we had to have things for "show and tell," to display during "circle time." The girls showed cute, stuffed toys or dolls with miniature trunks full of costumes. The boys brought remote-control cars or boats, and sometimes a small catcher's mitt. After family trips there were Mickey Mouses from Disneyland and transparent, plastic pens filled with bits of green money from the Treasury Department in Washington.

There wasn't much I could bring. My aunt in England sent me pretty tags from her teabags that had colorful birds and flowers printed on them. She wrote that although she had never met me in person, she knew I would appreciate such beautiful things. I loved thinking that every time she poured herself a cup of tea, she thought, "I'll send this lovely tag to Mia in the United States for her birthday." But the children in the circle looked at each other with raised eyebrows. Kids in my class would surely do the same if I ever managed to share our only family photo of olden times.

I came into the kitchen as Mom and Dad were drinking their tea. I had a plan to soften my request. First I would model my new invention, the tie. Then, quickly, I would slip in the request to borrow the photo, matter of factly, lightly.

"Mia," my mother asked, "What is that beautiful thing knotted on your neck?"

Though she didn't wear colors herself, she always noticed color combinations. She was considered an expert by those who bought her bags.

"Look, darling," she said to my father.

"I just finished it this evening with

my magic needle." I waved the crochet hook in front of her.

"I can't believe it," she said. "You are so quick, so smart! You have golden hands just like your grandmother."

My hands like my grandmother's? What else might I have from her? What was she like? Mrs. Searle promised we would learn amazing things from the photos. I had to try.

"Thanks, Mom. I really love it, too. But, uh, I need to ask you something. For Mrs. Searle's class we all need to bring in old photos of our families. As old as we can find. A special guest is coming to analyze them."

Mom's eyes opened wide and her hand fluttered to her mouth. She glanced toward the wall in the dining area and shook her head. She stared quietly while I held my breath till it hurt. Then she turned her white head back to me, her eyes brimming with tears.

"To take to school you want it? To maybe bend it or lose it? How can we do such a thing?"

Dad covered her hand with his and said, "Darling, you know Herman in the camera shop down the street we can trust. He could make a copy. Then Mia can take the copy to school. Him you can trust. He won't harm the picture."

"But the chemicals. If they spilled and there were nothing left. No. I can't."

Dad tried again. "Herman you can trust. He will understand. Myself, I will explain to him."

Mom finally shrugged, her head very low.

"If you like," she said.

3

As it turned out, I wore my striped tie the same day that I brought in the copy of the photo.

"Mia," many of the kids said, "Make me a tie, too. It's wild!"

Before the bell, the class traded photos. Most were black and white, showing smiling, laughing people in front of summer homes or around large, festive tables, decked with dainty china and delicate glasses.

"Mia," they said, "Why don't you show us yours?"

I held the small copy behind my back. It was so completely different from all the others. So serious.

"I can show you, but I don't know much about it," I said.

"Didn't you ask your parents? Didn't they explain it? Like my Dad told me all of my photos are from a summer place on Cape Cod. It's his favorite memory," Sharon said.

"Why should I ask? The guest speaker will tell us how to 'read' the photo. That should tell me something."

My friends glanced at each other with that look that said, "Weird!"

"Take your seats, please," Mrs. Searle tapped on the desk.

A thin stranger, tall enough to form an arch with his body as he bent over a small table, clicked a tray of slides into a gray projector. Mrs. Searle stepped closer and continued.

"For weeks we have been investigating our families' past. For some of you, this may turn out to be the most thrilling part of our detective work. All photographs tell a story in their own language. You can go over a photograph umpteen times and, if you know how, each time you will feel or learn something new. All you need are very sharp eyes and an expert in the field. Meet Mr. George Ahern."

Suddenly, all the shuffling of photos and papers stopped as Mr. Ahern turned toward his projector and motioned for Mrs. Searle to flick off the lights. A cheerful, wide, family photo appeared on the screen in front of the chalkboard. Older members of the family sat close together, leaning on each other. The young ones were grouped behind them, glancing in various directions.

"Read a photo the way you read a book—left to right and then down. Do that again and again, as you ask yourselves questions like these..."

"Mr. Ahern, please, it will be difficult for the class to write these questions in the dark. Can we go back to the photo after they have copied them?" asked Mrs. Searle.

Mr. Ahern pulled a sheaf of mimeographed papers from his briefcase on the floor.

"Actually, the questions are right here. I have a copy for each student. No doubt their parents will want to join them in their detective work."

This is how the sheet looked:

QUESTIONS FOR PHOTOANALYSIS

– What do you see immediately?

– Is something happening in this photo?

– What about the background? Can you tell if it is real or fake?

– Do the people seem close or distant from each other?

– If they are close, are they touching? How?

—How is each person feeling? Can you tell if
  the characters are confused or proud or fear-
  ful or angry or bored?

—If it is a group, can you tell if anyone has the
  power?

—Look at every part of the bodies. Does the
  expression of the mouth match the person's
  posture, for example?

—Can you identify with anyone in the photo? If
  so, how are you alike or how different?

—How do you feel about what you see?Does
  something you see disturb you?

  *To help you in your detective work, here
  are some details that you need to note:*

—Describe exactly what you see and include
  things that appear along with people. Write
  this down.

—Look again, this time more carefully, at those
  things and note their condition. Are houses in
  good repair? Is clothing appropriate?

—Can you tell where and when the photo was
  taken?

  I think all of us would have been
happy to pore over our photos with
questions in hand, to really get the hang

of this thing called photoanalysis, but Mr. Ahern switched his projector back on and analyzed the photo on the screen.

When he finished, he had two last suggestions that he had learned from a famous photoanalyst.

"Get yourself a partner," he said. "Have your partner ask you questions about your photo—try to find someone who knows very little about your background. This will help you see things you might not have noticed."

I liked his last suggestion best, although it frightened me.

"Imagine that a moment after this photo was snapped, the people started to move and speak. How would they look, what would they say? What would happen next?"

What had happened next, soon after my photo was taken? I really was afraid to know for sure.

By now, the whole class clamored to get to their own photos. We were supposed to bring in several. Now I was glad that I only had one to concentrate on.

I stared at the photo in the privacy of my desk. Mom sits center front in the photo, her blond hair combed smoothly to the side, her lips pursed together. A crisp looking, scalloped, white collar tops her plaid dress.

Mom's Mutti sits on the left, looking straight ahead with a blank stare. Her lips are pressed together in a straight line. She wears no make-up, but a lacy collar tucked in at the neckline decorates her dark dress.

Standing close behind and next to her is a young, wavy-haired boy, dressed in a dark, double-breasted jacket, studded with brass buttons in double rows. His hand grasps at my mother's arm, as though he is protecting her. His expression is grim.

Behind my mother stands a young boy with sleek, light hair. His face is handsome and his eyes seem to smile slightly. A pointed white collar peeks out from under a sweater of variegated wool. His hands are held behind his back.

Papa, Mom's father, is seated on the right. He wears a pinstriped suit, white shirt and tie, printed with zigzag patterns of light and dark. Papa looks old, perhaps because he is balding and because his light eyebrows are furrowed over angry eyes. His short, grayish beard does not hide facial muscles which look clenched, as though he might be trembling with fear or anger.

All of the people in the photo are close enough to touch each other, but none of them looks at another. The background is a dull smudge of brownish color.

The picture bothers me because,

except for the young, handsome, blond boy, it is totally grim. It seems strange that a family would pose in this finery without the tiniest shred of joy in their faces.

I don't know how long it took me to go over that photo just one time. I didn't hear the bell that signaled the end of class, but when I finished, I looked up to find Mrs. Searle leaning over my shoulder. Everyone else had vanished.

"Mia," she said, "I think your photo is one of the most mysterious and unusual in the class. Can you get more information from your parents?"

How could she understand the pain this photo caused my mother? How could she know how Dad and I avoided any mention of such matters around Mom so that she would not be reminded of what she lost? I just nodded.

"Maybe."

I was late for work at the yarn shop.

I jumped up quickly, tucked the photo into my bag and waved good-bye.

Irene had just received a shipment of thick, textured wool skeins of yarn in heathery colors. She wanted me to arrange them attractively in round, ice-cream canisters nailed to the wall. They gave a honeycomb effect and looked irresistible when filled with the new skeins. I hurried so I could show her my photo and my new tie invention.

She hadn't noticed the tie under my coat as I came in, but now as I climbed the ladder, she blinked her eyes and said, "Oh, Mia, I recognize my mohair. What a great idea!"

I told her how everyone in school wanted one just like it, and suddenly realized it would be wonderful for Irene if she could schedule crochet classes so that the kids, themselves, could make them.

"Why don't *you* give a class like that?

Saturday afternoons would be perfect," Irene said.

"No, I could never do that on a Saturday afternoon. We are pretty serious Sabbath observers. I love to crochet and I think it is restful, but it is simply not allowed."

"Really? What can you do on Sabbath in your home?" Irene seemed genuinely interested.

"Well, we have slow, festive meals where we catch up on everyone's news and we sing special Sabbath table songs. Mom's family had fantastic voices and loved to collect samples from all over the world. She knows dozens by heart!"

"And after the meals? What are you allowed to do?"

"After meals we take walks or naps or get into nice, fat library books. My Dad usually studies the Bible."

Irene smiled and nodded, then raised a finger with an idea.

"I've got it, Mia. Last week you told me you needed something for the Heirloom Fair at school. How about one of the songs from your Mom's family? It's wonderful that after all she suffered, she still observes the Sabbath and loves to sing."

It was an amazing thought. That there might be a shred left of Mom's home life. But for the fair I needed something that everyone could touch and understand. It wouldn't mean much to my friends and their parents to hear me sing in Hebrew. I wanted something that would amaze everyone.

"Maybe," I told Irene. "Maybe. And maybe we can have a crochet class another day."

4

It was already dark and chilly as I raced back to my parents' store to see whether I should set "milk" or "meat." The bell jangled as I entered. Two pink spots stood out on Mom's white face from the steam heat. She really looked beautiful.

"Hi, Mia, last week you invented the tie. Today I invent new bags. Very small and very large. Look here."

She had sewn a tiny bag that could be filled with something precious and had attached it to a silken cord. Then she drew it carefully over my head.

"Could be to show off or to hide something, no?" she whispered as she fingered the pendant.

"Now look here. For Daddy, a deluxe garment bag in beautiful fabric to give to special customers who love to travel elegantly. Well?"

I told her they were gorgeous.

"We'll talk later, Mia. Dad is hungry and you are sure hungry, too. Go and set for a milk meal and we will be up soon."

While I heated the tuna casserole and set the table, I glanced around, trying to imagine friends sitting in the living room for crochet class. With baskets of colorful yarn perched everywhere and a bunch of the kids cross-legged on the floor and couch, they would hardly notice how grim everything looked. Best of all, Mom could help them choose amazing color combos. At dinner that night Mom and Dad seemed happier than usual.

"Your Mom really helped someone today." Dad said. "Remember Mrs. Chase? One of her daughters is very, very sick, but the family will not give up hope. Today Mrs. Chase bought one of Mom's bags—a small delicate one with a long strap. And when Mom asked, 'What will you put in?' she said, "Dreams. Dreams of the future. Hopes.' She will hang the bag on her child's bedpost and fill it with scraps of paper—a different dream on each."

Mom took over the telling.

"All year I have not heard an answer like this. Even while she is so sick, her daughter dreams of the future and plans. And she has lost so much. So much strength, so much time," she said thoughtfully.

It seemed an incredibly good time to ask about the crochet class and the story behind the photo.

"Anytime," Mom answered when I

asked about the class. She actually looked excited about it.

"And one other thing," I said. "Mrs. Searle wants to know more about our photo. Is there more that you can tell me?"

Mom was quiet for a moment. Her fingers slowly traced over the figures in the photo. Then she kissed her fingers, closed her eyes and swayed from side to side.

"It's time to tell you what I can remember. The picture was taken right before Kurt's Bar Mitzvah. He is the one who stands next to Mutti. For days we walked kilometers without proper shoes, without warm coats—just as they caught us and deported us, hungry and frightened. When Mutti thought it was close to sundown, she put on her lace collar to honor the Sabbath. In Europe we washed and changed the collars of our clothing, not so much the clothing.

Then it was Sabbath and, somehow, we found a house that was like a shul, you know, a synagogue. In that shul my brother was called to the Torah and we felt—just for that moment—special and dignified. Can you see Mutti's lacy collar and how straight she sits in the photo?"

"And then, Mom, and then what happened?"

Now she rubbed her temples slowly with the balls of her fingers and closed her eyes.

"What happened? I don't know. We were separated. I only know that we separated for a while. I was sent to work as a maid for a Polish Jewish family. They were sent to the ghetto and from there, just like that, nothing left. I don't know if you want to tell your teacher all that."

I would wait to see. Mom had never said so much, so I pressed on with my questions.

"Remember, Mom, you said I had

golden hands like my grandmother?"

"*Ya*, right, darling. Really golden."

"And we have all the songs that you have always sung on the Sabbath…that we sing now.…"

Now she stopped rubbing and opened her eyes wide.

"*Ya, richtig,* right."

"So there is something left. Only a very little, but something. Right? Mom?"

"There is something. There is a lot, really, but it is so hard to think again of it, to remember hard, to build again in the mind."

Then she held out her hands, rubbing her thumbs against the balls of her fingers, squeezing hard.

"But nothing left to touch, to hold of them."

Gently Dad put down his teacup and covered Mom's tiny hands with his own.

"It will be better soon, darling."

At that moment I burst into tears. Not because my parents had confirmed the fact that there was absolutely nothing to show at the Heirloom Fair. It really wasn't that at all. Just at that moment I understood how impossible it would be for me to survive if I ever lost these dear people who loved me, and each other, so much.

And Mom had lost everyone! I felt terribly helpless and then frightened that watching me cry my parents would not tell me these stories anymore. They would think I couldn't bear to hear them. So I was perfectly honest and explained, "I could never be as brave as you. Never."

Mom touched my cheek lightly.

"We never know what we can do. We just do. We stand straight and we move in small steps."

5

The next day, I told Irene what Mom and I had planned for the crochet class.

"That's great, Mia. Today we'll collect all the odd balls and odd lots of yarn. You will have a regular smorgasbord of choices. I would be happy to help, but one of us has to mind the store. I know you can handle the groups. Needles we have, too. Let me see here."

Irene raked through a flat box of old steel, plastic, and aluminum hooks. I looked at her stiff, swollen fingers and thought how my grandmother's hands had never had a chance to grow old. Golden hands.

"Irene, we talked a little last night. I want you to know there is more left of our family than Sabbath songs. Mom said I have my grandmother's golden hands."

"Golden hands, you say," and she smiled. "In my family it was my great grandmother who had golden hands. Sit for a moment, Mia. The story of her golden hands will explain a lot about this shop.

"More than one hundred years ago, the most beautiful country in the world suffered the worst famine in the history of the world. My family lived in that land—Ireland. Nearly overnight they watched their potato plants sicken and die of a disease that spread like a plague.

"Have you learned in school, Mia, what is the perfect food? They knew it then. It was the potato, and they really taught the world how to make the most luscious mashed potatoes with butter and milk. But those poor, lovely people had only their small potato patches. At first some ran out to their field to scrabble under the earth, to pray that the blight had not reached beneath the stalks. Mostly, they found blackened, stinking lumps of decay.

"Children begged their parents for food and chewed the bark of trees and grasses that grew wild. The simple, good-hearted families tried to help each other but could not raise the rent for their thatch-roofed shacks. Their landlords preferred to burn down the shacks rather than allow them a grace period. Very soon, even the closest friends and relatives had nothing at all to give each other. Some tried to flee and used the last of their money to buy steerage tickets."

"And your family?" I asked.

"My family could not bear to leave. They walked to other villages, hoping to barter work for food. What they found was unimaginable: corpse-like bodies, whimpering, half-frozen under lean-to shelters that they had dragged together while they still had a bit of energy in them. So our family walked on to Cork.

"My great-grandmother was a young girl like you. She wanted so desperately to help feed her parents who could barely lift themselves off their straw pallets. They watched as the healthy grains and meat that Ireland produced were shipped off to Britain, while the Irish starved; but they also knew that the British were hungry for luxurious laces like the ones that were treasured in France and Italy. The rich and famous wore them.

"Finally great-grandmother went to classes in crochet that the nuns offered. It seemed totally crazy. The Irish villagers who managed to survive wrapped rags around their bones while the nuns spoke of making lace. In the end, they were very wise.

"For my great-grandmother, it was a privilege to go to the convent for her lessons. It was clean there and quiet. The only sound was the swishing of the sisters' long habits as they marched their apprentices to the workroom and the washroom because they needed clean hands to handle the fine, cotton thread and to learn the delicate workmanship. The nuns were demanding but kind, too; when the long hours in the stone-cold convent made their students tremble, they even provided sweaters.

"The nuns actually taught them how to produce small pieces of what we call Irish Crochet. It was difficult at first for stiff, cold fingers to work the threads, but mistakes were not disasters, because, as you know, mistakes in crochet can easily be pulled out.

"If the students did a really fine job, the nuns would sell the lace for them and provide money for precious, rare bread and corn. That is exactly what my great-grandmother did. She used finer and finer threads, and needles that were so slender, she could barely see the hook on the end.

"It was never easy. She could not continue to work at home after dark in the dim candlelight. Her eyes grew sore and she stabbed her fingers over and over again with the fine point of the hook. First she perfected the net-like grounding, and then the dainty but sturdy roses and leaves worked over cording.

"She eventually made beautiful lace. Not as fancy or complicated as the kind made in France or Italy, but lace, nevertheless. It was lace that would sell for collars and cuffs and romantic nightgowns. She did save the family, and none of them left Ireland until my mother came here to marry my dad."

"So it was the crochet hook, the noble needle, that helped to feed your family?"

"It was, Mia."

Irene picked up a fine, steel hook from the flat box.

"A needle just like this, and, of course, a lot of work."

"Do you know how to do it, Irene?"

"Oh, I can show you," she said, "but these swollen fingers trip over fine work."

Lace, I thought. Lace like the curtains in the cafe. Lace like the stiff version on the ruff around the neck of Queen Elizabeth I. Lace like you see in royal French portraits. Like the lace of Mutti's collar in our photo. I knew I needed to know how to do it.

6

Six, altogether, wanted to come over to make ties. It would be the first time any of them had ever come to our tiny apartment. Everyone else lived in large developments away from Central Avenue.

I worried what they would think. Whether they would feel sorry for us, that they would think Mom was strange. Added to everything else, Mom wanted to serve tea and cakes. They would expect cola and chips.

In the end, we scattered boxes of

yarn balls all around the living room and had the kids sit on the floor to work. I started with fat yarn and thick needles to teach the basic chain and single crochet. It was all they needed for the time being.

Lynn and Tom learned quickly. In less than half an hour they were ready to choose their colors for brightly striped ties. Mom showed them all kinds of possibilities while I worked with Kevin, Sharon, and David.

"What do you like?" she asked as she tossed various colors into the air.

Lynn thought rose, violet, and turquoise, but Tom hesitated.

"Grays and blues, I think," he said.

Mom nodded and then showed them how even the placement of the colors could change the total effect.

"That's amazing," Tom said.

I watched out of the corner of my eye as I practiced the simple stitches over and over with the slower ones.

Quietly, Mom walked around to offer colors to all my friends. They seemed pleased, and each held at least three different balls in their laps.

Moments later, everyone began on the narrow end of the tie, working back and forth in thick stripes. It was not all smooth crocheting, but mistakes could be pulled out easily and reworked.

Tom called me over.

"Is there a way to leave spaces between stitches—like a webbing or net?" he asked.

"Why, Tom, as a matter of fact, it's something I'm working on."

"Well this is going to sound weird, but my grandfather on my mother's side was an Ojibway Indian. I'm planning to bring in a dreamcatcher that we inherited from him."

"A dreamcatcher?" the others chorused. "What on earth?"

"I was going to wait until our Heirloom Fair to talk about it, but here goes. My grandfather's family hung a willow branch bent into the shape of a fish, and webbed with thread strung with beads, feather, and bits of leather, above the cradles of their little ones to trap bad dreams. The good dreams could pass right through the center of the web.

"I thought I might try to copy it in all kinds of colors, possibly using crochet for the webbing, that is, if Mia will help me. I could give them to people I care about to help improve their nights."

"Oh, Tom," Sharon said, "How wonderful! I want one. I'm ordering it right now."

Out of the corner of my eye, I watched Mom. She was definitely listening. Somehow I thought she would need a dreamcatcher cast from webbed steel.

Toward the end of the evening, Mom

handed out brown lunch bags to hold the work safely, and served tea and cake on our plain, wooden, kitchen table.

I kept worrying that my friends would think the food was weird, that they would laugh at the queerness of our ways. So I was shocked when Lynn whispered, "You're really lucky, Mia. Your mom is a color genius and she's nice. My mom would never take this much time to do anything with me or my friends. And we're lucky to have you for a friend."

David loved the cake.

"It's kosher, isn't it? That's why it's so delicious, probably."

Mom winked at me.

It was 9:00 PM and no one wanted to leave. They needed help in increasing stitches so that the ties could grow gradually wider at the other end. I also taught them how to tuck in and hide the yarn ends.

Everyone continued working comfortably on the floor and talk turned to the upcoming Heirloom Fair. David had an ancient samovar from his grandmother in Russia that he was hoping to be allowed to display. Karen planned on bringing an old Christian Bible with generations of her family inscribed on its tattered endpapers.

Mom cleared the small, wooden table and draped it with towels. Then she helped those who had finished steam the bumps out of their gorgeous ties.

It was very late once they left. It had been a great evening, and Mom had made it great. Poor Dad was still working downstairs.

My fingers were feeling tired but itchy—impatient for some special project. It was strange. My fingers knew before I did that there was work to be done.

7

There were three cartons of new, imported yarn to unload before Irene and I had time to talk and crochet. I wanted to know more about Irish Crochet. I wanted to try it.

Before we actually started to practice, Irene showed me photos of various groundings. They were like webbing or netting, but with beautiful picots or regularly spaced ornamental loops and knots, that made the piece look much more elegant and feminine than fishnet or a dreamcatcher!

Irene had the cream-colored thread that I needed and the needle, but I struggled with the tiny loops. How did Irene's young, great-grandmother ever master this skill at all?

First I just tried regular stitches in miniature, then the large, lacy spaces that make up the Irish Crochet background. The holes were uneven and my fingers were cut with wrongheaded stabs of the needle. All the nubs or picots were different sizes and lay in different directions. I wondered if I could ever master this lace if my family's life depended on it!

Irene laughed when I said that.

"Oh, Mia, it takes a lot of practice—of course you could. But, thank God, you don't have to. Take this home. Just relax with it. By the way, I already have three new customers, thanks to your tie session. Some of your friends came. Even one fellow."

"It wouldn't have been as great an evening without your yarn and needles. We couldn't have done it at all," I reminded her.

"The new people spoke of your mother's wonderful eye for color. They liked the whole project because you showed them it could be done and because it just plain feels good."

What felt good was the new me in school. My friends thought my Mom was some kind of exotic, European designer. They actually loved our home, too.

"Your apartment," they said, "is so classy and bare. Why you could come home every day and redesign the decor. It would be like moving into a new home every day. Infinite possibilities. And beige. It's ever so sophisticated."

So things were looking up at school but I still had not solved my problem of what to bring for the Heirloom Fair, and there was less than one week left.

During lunch the next day, Ted, Sharon, and Lynn talked about their projects. Sharon was bursting with excitement.

"I can't wait to show it to you. It's a quilt that my great-great-grandmother wept over and stitched slowly (so says my dad) on blustery, winter days when the wind howled over the Nebraska prairie. There was just enough light to see and too much snow to budge the door open for regular chores."

Sharon pushed her tray aside and gestured with her arms, rubbing them with her fingers.

"Can't you just imagine that? All of them bundled up in heavy sweaters, the quilt on their laps, and no one else to talk to for miles around. What courage that must have taken! The only link with the outside was a rope that great-great-grandfather rigged up from the back door to the barn so that he could find his way to the cows."

"Does the quilt look old and worn?" David asked.

"Yes, but we've done some stitching here and there to make it stronger. You'll soon see. But I can't make my stitches as tiny as my great-great-grandmother could, no matter how hard I try."

David said he was spending his evenings polishing up a pot-bellied samovar that had been shipped, all dented and tarnished, from Tula in the Soviet Union.

"The part of all this that was brand new for me was that you don't plunk it down on a stove. It's not just another teapot. The Russian samovar we inherited has a special pipe right down the center that they used to fill with charcoal and wood."

David picked up his napkin and began to polish the glass on his tray.

"It's amazing," he said. "Every evening I can't wait to polish it. For me, it's like Aladdin's lamp. I can almost hear some of the conversations in the old village that this samovar heard as it bubbled away on a sideboard. I can almost see the generations of tea drinkers sipping tea through sugar cubes. The thing really speaks to me."

It was Lynn's turn now.

"Wait till you hear me on our Russian balalaika! Violin lessons finally paid off. I can tune this instrument the same way and I don't need to bother with rosin on a bow. There is no bow!"

"So it's like a guitar?" David asked.

"It has frets like a guitar but with a shorter neck, and it has three sets of double strings. But it's much smaller than a guitar—at least ours is—and it has a triangular body."

"So you strum it?"

"Mostly you pluck it. But I've got

some problems I hope I can solve by Tuesday. First of all, one string is missing. My music teacher is trying to help me figure something out."

"No big deal, Lynn," David laughed.

"Wait, you haven't heard the biggest problem yet. You don't just play a balalaika. You sing with it. The Russians sang all the time—in boats, on the street, in trains, in restaurants, and on benches pushed up to the front of their houses. They sang in groups of at least two or three together. Sometimes they added an accordion."

"So you'll sing for us?"

"I'll try. I'm learning a folksong about a horseman, but Tuesday is bearing down on me as heavily as that horseman!"

Tuesday. No samovar, no quilt or balalaika. Nothing to polish or tune or repair. Nothing you could touch. Nothing?

8

That evening before Sabbath, I stopped at Irene's shop just long enough to pick up an extra ball of fine thread for practice on the Irish work. It would keep me busy after the Sabbath.

On Friday evenings I usually set the table and put the food in the oven so that Mom and Dad, coming up from the shop, could shower and dress before sunset.

Later, with the candles lit and the challah and wine blessed, we would slowly eat and sing *zemirot,* Sabbath table songs, between courses. Dad told us that even in his home, his mother always required that the company sing before the next course was served. Maybe Mom's songs attracted Dad to her because they were sweet and very beautiful.

When we sang, I imagined molecules of sound like delicately tinted soap bubbles, floating around us—from deep purple to tinkly silver. Dad and I learned Mom's songs by heart and even tried to harmonize.

There were all kinds of songs from all over the world. One sounded like an Irish jig and another imitated the special gait of a camel in a Middle Eastern desert.

When special guests visited us on the Sabbath, we always asked them to teach us a new song rather than bring flowers or wine. We especially loved exotic, new (for us) ones from far-off lands.

Irene was right. The *zemirot* were heirlooms. If need be, if time ran out, I could present one or two, talk about them, where they came from, how the world over, no matter what the situation, Jews sing out the praises of the Sabbath—a small piece of peace. I could pass out mimeographed sheets with the translations. I could even teach a simple one to the audience.

On the other hand, the audience wouldn't see those bubbles of joy that surround us every Sabbath evening. My voice isn't Mom's voice. No one at the Heirloom Fair could feel the specialness of the Sabbath. They couldn't smell it or touch it. Oh Lord! What could I do?

By now Dad was bringing in the spiced apple pie and Mom, the teacups. As if noticing for the first time, Dad suddenly looked at her and said, "You look beautiful tonight, darling, but you need something with that suit—a necklace or scarf, something there at the neck."

In that instant, at a dizzying speed, I glanced back and forth from Mom to Mutti in the photo behind her. Mutti's collar. Just such a lace collar would be perfect on Mom's suit!

Tom's words came back to me.

"I thought I'd try to copy my grandfather's dreamcatcher."

If Tom could copy such an heirloom, why couldn't I? I could crochet a lace collar. I could tell its story for the Heirloom Fair. How Mutti cared enough to wear it just days before she was shot outside the ghetto, how it displayed her dignity to the last moment.

But could I?

Could I design a simple triangle to tie like a scarf at the neck? Could I keep the spaces even, the picots all the same size and leaning in the right direction? Could I learn to stop stabbing my fingers so that drops of blood would not stain the work? But, most of all, could I finish the piece in time? This was already Friday night. The Heirloom Fair would be held on Tuesday evening.

The next day was Sabbath; all day. No needlework permitted. No real planning either.

But once Mom and Dad settled in for their Sabbath afternoon naps, I examined Mutti's collar in the photo with a magnifying glass. It was definitely lace. It could have been similar to the Irish Crochet grounding that Irene showed me. In any case, tucked into the neckline, no one would notice the lack of fancier stitches or roses.

The picot-decorated, net-like grounding would do. I could imagine a triangle of it, trimmed with picots all around.

My own nap was anything but restful. Cousin Marta had once told Dad horrifying details about "the end." The strange thing is that I don't remember hearing them. But now the drama played itself out in a dream.

Marta had told Dad that before Mutti and the children were shot, they were forced to undress at the edge of a huge pit. In my dream I was there.

First, I see them approaching the pit in a broad line. They only hear the shots and screams, unable to imagine what awaits them. The children cling to Mutti, trembling with fear. The Nazis scream, "Faster, faster!" Mutti pries their arms away from her waist and shoulders and helps them, gently, to undress.

"Faster, faster!"

Then Mutti sees to herself. She has never undressed in front of the children, so she starts with her shoes and stockings. Then she steps out of her dress and her underwear, onto the sharp stones and twigs. The cold bites and there is screaming. The children claw at her bare skin. Her fingers flutter to her collar. It is the last piece to drop onto the blood-soaked earth, slowly, slowly like those slow-motion sequences in the movies. And then?

I woke up on a tear-stained pillow. Irene had teased that I was lucky my life didn't depend on mastering Irish Crochet. Now I felt as though it did.

After the Sabbath we sang the *Havdala*, a prayer recited over wine, candle, and spices. I thought about how every Saturday night we sing of Elijah the Prophet who will some day bring good news of lasting peace. Every week, a fresh prayer, but always the same wish.

In our little world, in our tiny apartment, there was a bit more peace. Mom talked more. She walked with a lighter step; the nights were better. A little better.

After *Havdala*, Mom and Dad went down to the shop to catch up on work and I struggled with the baseline chain of the lace. I had to figure out how long the base of the triangle would have to be to hang properly at the neckline. Then, how many motifs or hole patterns per inch to figure on. How gradually would I need to decrease to the point of the triangle?

This was nothing like the instant tie project. The thread was fine, the hook on the needle was barely large enough to see, and the number of stitches in the hundreds, at least at the base.

After three hours of work, the triangle was two inches high. It didn't help that every twenty minutes I had to stop work to scrub my fingers that got tense and damp. The work had to be kept absolutely clean since there was no time to wash and dry it.

By Sunday afternoon, there was nothing left of Irene's thread and none of the shops would be open until

Monday. I still did have to go to school, so everything started to look hopeless, once again.

"Irene!" I shouted frantically, as I burst through the door that Monday after school.

"I need thread! I need help! I need time!"

"Mia, what is it? What has happened?"

Carefully I spread the work on the counter. I told her everything, tripping over words, frantic to get the thread and hook back into my hand.

On the counter the unfinished triangle looked wobbly and weak, some of the edges rough and knobby.

"Look, Mia," she said. "Finish the triangle now. You're working toward the point of the triangle; every row has fewer stitches. It won't take long now. The rows will go faster and faster."

"But what about your cases of yarn?

Who will unpack today?"

"They'll wait, Mia. If I remember correctly, this is probably a back-up order. The stuff we sell all the time, in basic colors. I don't think it's anything new and exciting."

I sat down behind the counter to work. Irene handled a few customers, but I did not look up once. I was counting, stretching, rubbing my sore fingertips, flicking the hook in and out of the tiny holes, fast.

"When you get to the point, don't snip the thread," Irene warned.

By the time I reached the point of the triangle, I ached everywhere, my neck, my shoulders, my head. Irene took the piece and spread it out over the black marble counter. It was not a pretty sight. The edges were lumpy, the picots, slightly uneven, and the stitches, not uniformly delicate and neat. It looked like what it was: a beginner's piece. I might still have to resort to the table songs.

Before I knew what was happening, Irene grabbed the hook, and with her swollen fingers, working flat on the countertop, she crocheted a row of single crochet with picots every quarter of an inch or so, around all three edges of the triangle. Magically, the edges grew smooth and elegant.

When it was finished, she tied it around my neck and I kissed her.

"It's wonderful, Mia. A wonderful idea and a wonderful product. Let's spray it gently with water and steam it lightly so that it will look really finished."

While we worked, she asked me more about the big fair.

"First of all," I told her, "you've got to be there!"

"Are you worried about how your mom and dad will react? This will be a shock for them, don't you think?"

"I hope they'll like this idea. I think they will."

But while Irene searched for a suitable box and tissue paper, I began to worry.

First of all, the dreamcatcher Tom was bringing in for the Heirloom Fair was genuine, generations old. He would copy it later for friends, not for the fair. My heirloom was basically counterfeit.

Could I make everyone understand that what I inherited from Mutti was real? It was what the lace collar stood for: her dignity and faith in the face of terror, her special brand of pride.

But, most of all, maybe Irene was right. Maybe seeing that collar would bring all the terror back to Mom.

Would she finger it with wonder and think, "My *gebenschte kind!* My blessed child! Now there is something to touch and to hold." Or would she look at it in horror and weep bitter tears again?

I was gambling. It had taken so long for her to be better.

Irene's voice broke into my thoughts.

"Here it is, Mia, as though it's been restored by a real pro."

Irene opened a smallish, shallow box filled with pale blue tissue. The creamy lace lay inside, folded neatly.

"Now you'll just have to figure out what to say about it," she smiled.

I hugged her hard and cried a little.

9

Tuesday morning before school, Dad remembered first. He rinsed out his coffee cup and faced me.

"Mia, tonight is the fair, yes?"

"Um hm," I answered him as I balanced a soft egg on my slice of rye.

"We all go together, right?"

"About 7:00."

"But Mia, we have given you nothing to take. What…" Mom was already wiping the counters.

"Don't worry, Mom. I'll figure out something. There will be so many heirlooms and stories; no one will notice..."

"Well then, tonight we eat at 6:00 and go after."

We stayed after school late that afternoon to set up. The halls were nearly vibrating with excitement. Mrs. Searle needed help arranging our photos on a special display in the auditorium. Mine was so quiet among the others. So gray.

Mrs. Searle had really thought of everything. She had music playing in the background: Spanish guitars, Russian balalaikas, German violins, and Scottish bagpipes.

In a far corner of the auditorium colorful finger foods decorated long tables. Maria Theresa's parents patted fresh tortillas into shape right on the spot. While we stood amazed at how quickly their hands and fingers worked the dough, she said, "We are these tortillas. At home in Guatemala we ate them all day long, breakfast, lunch, and supper."

"Do you still eat them so often here?" someone asked.

"Well, maybe not quite as often. I'm liking pizza now and even Chinese food."

Katherine arranged special, lacy Greek pastries on trays and David stacked pitas and falafel balls in large wooden bowls.

I thought about Irene. If she were a student or parent here, she could fill a whole table with potato delicacies: creamy mashed, herbed, scalloped, dumplings, and on and on.

"Hey you gluttons, over here!" Tom shouted.

He and the custodians snapped open folding chairs and lined them up in front of the stage which featured only a simple table and microphone for the heirloom presentations. We all helped for a while and then began to gather up our bags so we could make it home for a quick dinner before the program.

None of the heirlooms was on display in advance. Each one would be a surprise for all of the parents and most of the students.

I could barely swallow a morsel of dinner. Secretly, I glanced at my parents over and over. I was sure that they did not suspect a thing. I still wasn't sure what their reaction would be.

I thought of Mom in her purple dress, weeping and coughing over the photo so many years ago on this very table, of the terror-filled nights, and I prayed, I really prayed, that I was doing the right thing. That she would be ready. That there would be less pain, not more.

As it turned out, whole families jammed the entrance ways to the school: uncles, aunts, grandparents. But I felt OK, really strong and proud, walking between my parents—just the three of us.

Irene had called to say that she would be a little late, but she wouldn't miss the fair for the world.

Minutes before the program began, Mrs. Searle greeted us warmly.

"You must be Mia's mother. I recognize you from the photo she brought."

Mom's hand fluttered to her lips for a moment. Then she recovered.

"Oh, *ya*, the copy you mean. Can you really tell it is me?"

Mrs. Searle smiled and patted her arm.

"Absolutely. Please excuse me, we want to begin exactly on time."

We started by singing the national anthem. Mom and Dad stood very straight and faced the flag. Tears welled up in their eyes and then in mine. Were there others here tonight who could sing, "Oh say, does that star-spangled banner yet wave, o'er the land of the free and the home of the brave" with so much feeling?

Mrs. Searle described the course of study that covered Ellis Island, the family trees, and photoanalysis.

"You have all done such extraordinary work throughout the semester that I am waiting with bated breath to see and hear about your heirlooms."

She thanked the parents who had helped with the food and invited the audience to sample all the ethnic delicacies after the program.

"Without further ado, we shall begin."

There were a number of predictable kinds of heirlooms. Brian brought in a set of silver spoons from England. They were part of a tea set that had been handed down through five generations to Brian's mother, who stopped using them when she realized that a whole branch of her family had inherited very bad, soft teeth, probably from the gallons of sweet tea they had sipped.

To be fair, though, friends had asked, could they not also have resulted from the jams and breads and pastries that always accompanied the sweet tea? Most assuredly, she thought.

The audience laughed and Brian looked sheepish.

Sylvia showed the cap that her father had worn on ship deck as the liner steamed toward New York Harbor. The brim of the worn, brown, tweed cap had shaded his eyes as he craned his neck to catch a first glimpse of Lady Liberty.

Dad squeezed my hand and reached under his glasses to flick away a tear.

"Me too, Mia. Me too."

Karen displayed a tattered Bible—at least 150 years old—that her family used only for the inscription of new births. They were, she thought, a rare family that still followed such old fashioned customs.

Tom's dreamcatcher charmed the

audience. It was as warm and safe an Indian artifact as a peace pipe, but modern, too. If Tom really went into production, each family here would gladly order one, judging by the applause.

Sharon's quilt was thin and worn, but the details she shared about the challenging conditions on the Nebraska prairie added a lot of interest.

From where we sat, though, very few could appreciate her great-great-grandmother's tiny stitches.

David would have liked, he said, to heat up the wood in the central chamber of his samovar so that we could all hear the steamy bubbling that was background music in most Russian homes for generations.

Since he could not, he told us samovar trivia: that samovars were manufactured by the hundreds of thousands in Tula (where his came from) but that they were made in all shapes and sizes. Some were as huge as three to four feet high and others small enough to disassemble and carry on a train.

He had worked hard to make his samovar gleam, but would need professional help to get rid of all the dents, he said.

We were all anxious to hear Lynn on the balalaika which she had managed to fix up with her music teacher. It did not look easy, but she sounded terrific, if a bit slow.

It was, she said, a tall order to learn the Russian lyrics and balalaika playing technique—all in a few short weeks! So she had arranged for the audience to enjoy a really professional balalaika experience.

At her signal, Mrs. Searle switched on a recording of a balalaika orchestra. Lynn explained that balalaikas come in many sizes, from small violin size to bass viol.

Here was the Russian passion everyone had expected, starting slowly and
picking up momentum and volume. The
audience broke into rhythmic clapping
and nearly danced from their seats as
the music played on.

The last presentation before mine
was my favorite because it was incredibly earthy. Totally unexpected.

Anne said she came from real "poor
stock." She was the first in her entire
family to get past elementary school.
But she was a fifth-generation American
and proud of it. She was also proud of
the little tin box she held up for our
inspection.

The tin was so worn that it was
impossible to tell what colors had once
been printed on it. Anne opened it carefully, revealing a bar of white soap, a
bottle of baby oil, nail clippers, and a
few white, threadbare, terry washcloths.

These, she told us, were the tools

that a great-great-aunt who was called "the bath lady" used in her work. This was the story:

Before her husbands died, she had nursed them, one after the other. She got used to bathing them when it was "high time," and the last one said she had "sympathetic hands" that would "ease him right to heaven."

When he died, leaving her penniless, she looked down at those "sympathetic hands" and thought, "Why not? Why not give baths professionally?"

"So that was exactly what she did," Anne said. "My family claims she could work on sorry patients, real bags of bones, and restore them to a healthy glow with those sympathetic hands.

"Who knows? Maybe I'll be the next to try," Anne said as she clicked the lid back down.

Sympathetic hands, golden hands, and noble needles, I thought playfully, and then realized it was my turn. This is what I said.

"Some of you know that I was very nervous about tonight because I thought our family had no heirlooms. In the end, I could have brought so much. I could have sung table songs that our family has been collecting for generations. I could have told you about our calendar, so full of holidays and special occasions, and about how good and strong our family is.

"Someday maybe our family will be able to remember happy things, funny things that happened before the war. Someday, when it doesn't hurt so much to remember."

Then I opened the flat box lined with tissue paper.

"This is what I finally chose. I made this lace collar to match the one my grandmother wore in the last and only photo we have of her. In the photo it is difficult to see, but I think it must have looked something like this."

Someone in the audience coughed.

"You must be thinking that I have not really fulfilled the assignment. After all, you can't just manufacture an heirloom on the spot, although heirlooms have to start somewhere. It has to be handed down.

"So let me explain. My grandmother was deported from her home and became a refugee on the run, still she managed to change her collar for the Sabbath of my uncle's Bar Mitzvah, only a short time before she and her children were shot. To me, her collar represents dignity and the will and courage she mustered to celebrate. Every time I glance at that photo, it is a sparkling lesson of how we need to stand proud.

"Mostly, though, I made this for my mother. She misses them all so much—her whole family—and wants something to be left that she can touch and hold."

When I glanced up to hold up the lace triangle, the crowd was reaching for handkerchiefs. Mom and Dad held tight to each other.

I tied it around my neck.

"This is how my grandmother wore it on that last Sabbath of her life—we know that from the photo snapped moments before that last, fateful Sabbath before her son's Bar Mitzvah, in a strange synagogue, miles away from her home.

"David told you how the samovar speaks to him." I touched the scarf around my neck. "When I wear this, I feel Mutti's—my grandmother's—strength and dignity and courage. I guess it works like an heirloom."

Before I could carefully untie the lace, the audience rose, one section at a time, clapping loudly, for a very long time.

Mrs. Searle, tears streaming from her eyes, came over and kissed me and, gently, led me off the stage. Then Irene (she came!) hugged me hard. Mom and Dad squeezed me and said, *"gebenschte kind!"* And everyone crowded around close to touch the lace and see how it was done.

How?

I winked at Irene.

I told them, "With love and a noble needle—but that's another story."

Mia's version of Mutti's lace collar.

Faye Silton was born in South Bend, Indiana, to Holocaust survivors. She graduated from Stern College and continued her Judaic and Hebraic studies at the Hebrew University in Jerusalem and the Jewish Theological Seminary in New York. Silton is a writer and educator, and lives in Albany, New York with her husband. They have seven children. This is her first novel.